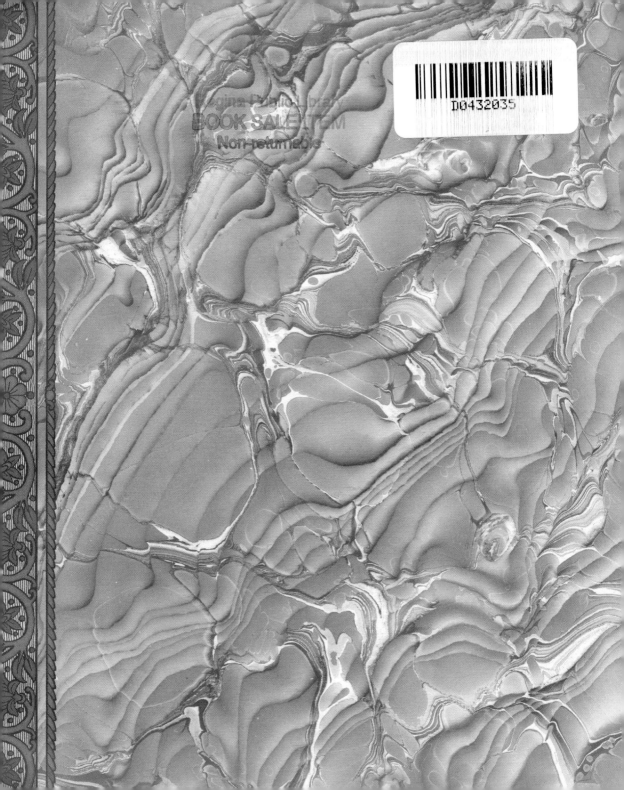

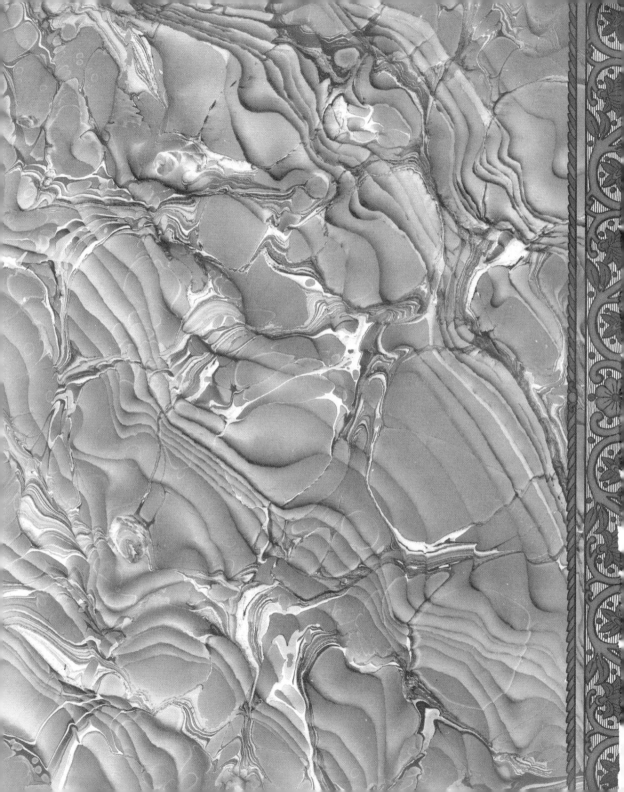

THE OCEANOLOGY HANDBOOK

A COURSE FOR UNDERWATER EXPLORERS

BY PROFESSOR PIERRE ARONNAX

edited by Clint Twist

CANDLEWICK PRESS
PUBLISHERS OF RARE & UNUSUAL BOOKS

Library of Congress Cataloging-in-Publication Data
Professor Arronax.
The oceanology handbook / Professor Arronax ; by Clint Twist.
p. cm.
ISBN 978-0-7636-4874-9
1. Oceanography—Juvenile literature. 2. Ocean—Juvenile literature. I. Twist, Clint.
GC21.5.P76 2010
551.46—dc22   2009047105

10 11 12 13 14 15 16 SLS 10 9 8 7 6 5 4 3 2 1
Manufactured in Shenzhen, Guangdong, China
www.ologyworld.com

CANDLEWICK PRESS
99 Dover Street
Somerville, Massachusetts 02144
www.candlewick.com

PUBLISHER'S NOTE

The manuscript of this book was found inside a watertight
container washed up among bits of wreckage on a remote Spanish
beach in 1863. It seems to have remained in the finder's family for
some time—more, we suspect, for its curiosity value and the
novelty of its illustrations than for its text (which was in French).
Years later, it ended up in a junk shop in Cádiz, where its
significance was recognised by a young man studying marine
biology at the University of Madrid. Whatever strange events were
witnessed by the author of these pages before his untimely demise,
there is no doubt that his insightful writing anticipated many later
discoveries. Some of the events described here seem to tie in with
the journal of Zoticus de Lesseps, which is available in a volume
entitled *Oceanology: The True Account of the Voyage of the Nautilus.*

TICKET

No. 87

Louis & Co.
73 rue de Seine,
Paris

Louis & Co.
29 esplanade de la Mer,
Marseille

NAMES	AGES	This ticket entitles the holder to passage on board the
		QUEEN HORTENSE
P. Aronnax	53	steamer from *MARSEILLE TO CÁDIZ*
		Departure
		3rd April 1863 at 12 noon

This ticket is valid only for the journey and person stated above.
Passengers are advised to arrive at least one hour prior to departure.

Signed on behalf of LOUIS & Co.

This ordinary steamer ticket was to lead to the most incredible voyage ever undertaken by a man of science.

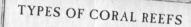

TYPES OF CORAL REEFS

Fringing reef

Barrier reef

Atoll

I have been able to confirm from my own observations the veracity of Mr. Darwin's theory as to the origin of coral atolls.

Mere words cannot begin to describe
the myriad wonders and peculiarities
of the underwater world.

CONTENTS

Dear Reader,

Earlier this year, in the company of Professor Ewing, the fisherman Ned Land, and a young assistant named Zoticus de Lesseps, I set out on an incredible voyage aboard a submarine known as the <u>Nautilus</u>, commanded by one Captain Nemo. Since April, we have travelled for thousands of miles beneath the world's oceans, under the very noses of ships bobbing unsuspectingly on the surface. We have seen sights that no human has ever before witnessed, and encountered many strange and sometimes frightening creatures. The advances in science made during this voyage have been truly astonishing.

The aim of this humble volume is to provide an accurate account of the world's oceans, drawing together the various strands of underwater research into a comprehensive course for young oceanologists. The book has been compiled as we have travelled with the assistance of Professor Ewing (the foremost expert in the field of marine geology) and with help from Ned Land, a seasoned ocean voyager. My area of expertise is that of marine biology— the study of the wondrous flora and fauna of the oceans.

Whilst the majority of these pages have been compiled in a mood of exhilaration about our incredible discoveries, the events of the last few days have caused a deep sense of foreboding as to the future of the voyage. Captain Nemo is so obsessed with the treasures of the ancient kingdom of Atlantis that he appears quite unhinged, and I am certain he means never to let us return home. I am so fearful about my fate that I am placing this manuscript in a sealed package with the earnest hope that if I myself do not survive, then at least the discoveries I have so far made will be preserved for future generations.

Yours in haste,
Professor Pierre Aronnax

PUBLISHER'S NOTE
The dramatic events alluded to above have been described in more detail in the aforementioned journal of Zoticus de Lesseps, entitled Oceanology: The True Account of the Voyage of the Nautilus.

There is nothing so thrilling as
departing on an ocean voyage.
There is always a delightful air of
anticipation on the waterfront.

PART 1

EXPLORING THE OCEANS

To begin our study of oceanology, I shall acquaint the reader with some introductory information about the oceans and explain the various means by which they are navigated and explored. Ocean exploration can be a perilous business, even on the surface, so I can only hope that our fate aboard the _Nautilus_ proves to be more favourable than that of captains Magellan, Cook, and La Pérouse.

The one-man submarine _Turtle_, built in 1775, was designed as a warship rather than an underwater exploration vessel.

CHAPTER 1

OCEANS OF THE WORLD

The oceans form a layer of salt water that covers about three-quarters of the Earth's surface and completely surrounds all the land.

Arctic Ocean: 5½ million square miles (14 million square km)

Atlantic Ocean: 31 million square miles (82 million square km)

Indian Ocean: 28 million square miles (73 million square km)

Pacific Ocean: 64 million square miles (165 million square km)

Southern Ocean: 7¼ million square miles (20 million square km)

North America

Gulf of Mexico

Pacific Ocean

Atlantic

South America

Strait of Magellan

The puffin (Fratercula arctica) is a brightly billed seabird found along the Atlantic coastlines of northern Europe.

SEAS, GULFS, BAYS, AND STRAITS

The huge oceans of the world can be divided into smaller regions. A *sea* is a large area of ocean that is partly enclosed by land. A *gulf* is also partly enclosed, while a *bay* is a smaller region that is formed by an indentation in a coastline. A *strait* is a narrow strip of ocean that separates two pieces of land.

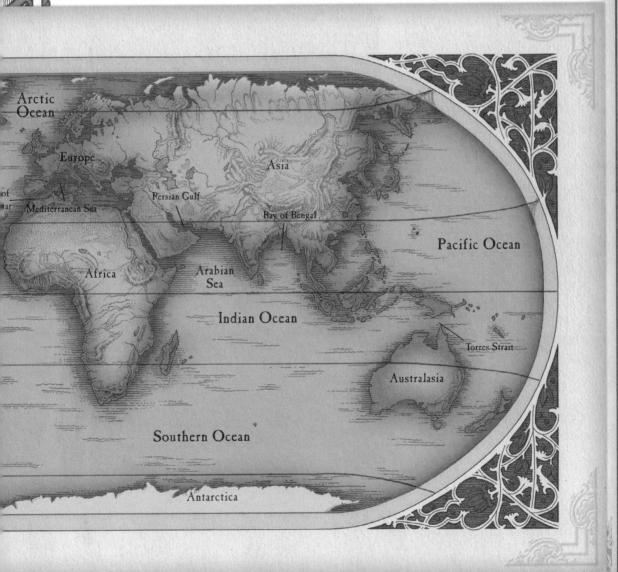

Arctic Ocean

Europe

Asia

of ar

Persian Gulf

Mediterranean Sea

Bay of Bengal

Pacific Ocean

Africa

Arabian Sea

Indian Ocean

Torres Strait

Australasia

Southern Ocean

Antarctica

CHAPTER 2
A BRIEF HISTORY OF SHIPS

People have been travelling the oceans for thousands of years. At first they used canoes made from hollowed-out tree trunks, or crude rafts built from strapped-together pieces of wood. Later, they learned how to make boats and ships by nailing together planks to form a hull. Any gaps between the planks were made watertight with tar or resin.

MUSCLE POWER

The very first boats were powered by people. Their crews used simple wooden paddles to move them forward through the water. The invention of oars made this task a bit easier. An oar is a long-handled paddle that can be levered against the side of the boat to produce more power.

WIND POWER

By adding upright masts and sails supported by wooden spars, shipbuilders were able to harness the wind to drive their ships forward. However, these sails were useful only when the wind was blowing in the right direction, so ancient sailing ships often had oars as well.

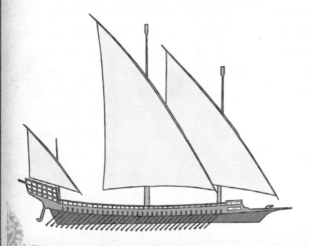

THE AGE OF SAIL

By the sixteenth century, people had learned to make ships that were capable of sailing around the world. Through a clever combination of masts, sails, and ropes (arranged in a network called the rigging), these ships were able to make their way across the oceans in almost any wind conditions.

STEAM POWER

At the beginning of the nineteenth century, coal-fired steam engines were used to power riverboats. However, by the 1850s, more powerful engines were being fitted to oceangoing ships.

These engines turn huge paddle wheels that power the ship through the water. However, these ships still carry a full set of sails in case they run out of coal.

ACTIVITY: Find out how to make a simple model sailing ship. You could use a piece of wood for the hull, a dowel for the mast, and a sheet of stiff paper for the sail.

Chapter 3

Navigation

Navigation is the science of going in the right direction. This feat is easy enough to achieve on land, where there are usually plenty of landmarks. At sea, however, it is much more difficult, especially when you are out of sight of land, so that there are no recognisable features in view.

Bird's-Eye View

Because the Earth has a curved surface, the higher up you are, the farther you can see. Therefore, in order to navigate successfully, one crew member must climb to the top of the mast to keep watch. The lookout platform on the tallest mast of a ship is called the crow's nest.

Telescopes

The telescope (invented in about 1608) is a great help to navigation at sea. This piece of equipment makes distant details clear by magnifying them through a series of glass lenses.

Sighting the Sun

The backstaff is the sailor's traditional device for measuring the height of the sun above the horizon. The backstaff is gradually being replaced by its modern equivalent, the sextant.

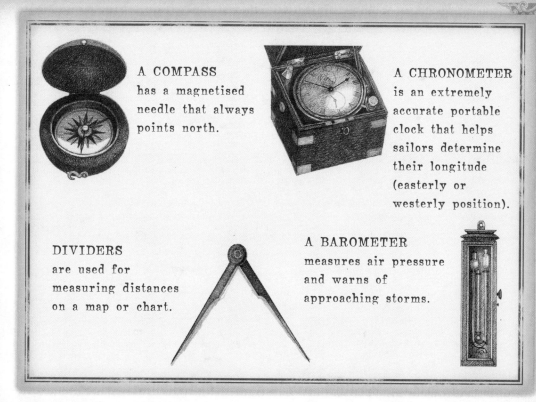

A COMPASS has a magnetised needle that always points north.

A CHRONOMETER is an extremely accurate portable clock that helps sailors determine their longitude (easterly or westerly position).

DIVIDERS are used for measuring distances on a map or chart.

A BAROMETER measures air pressure and warns of approaching storms.

SCIENTIFIC MEASUREMENT

Successful navigation means always knowing where you are. By measuring the height of the sun at a particular time of day, a ship's navigator can calculate his position fairly accurately and adjust the ship's course if necessary. If the navigator notices a sudden drop in air pressure on the barometer, he can prepare the ship for stormy weather.

ACTIVITY: A compass rose shows the main directions: north, south, east, and west. The angles between these points are divided and then divided again to produce sixteen directions. Compass points can be given in degrees, where north is 0°, east is 90°, south is 180°, and west is 270°. How many degrees is equivalent to west-southwest (WSW)?

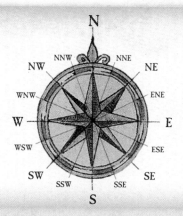

Chapter 4
Flags

At sea, flags are used for both identification and communication. A ship's flag, which is usually flown from the top of its mast, shows the nationality of the vessel. Smaller flags can be used to give specific information to other ships or to spell out messages, one letter at a time, in the semaphore code.

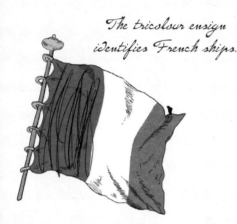

The tricolour ensign identifies French ships.

Friend or Foe?

Some countries have a special flag design for ships, while others use the national flag on their vessels. In both cases, the flags flown from ships are known as jacks or ensigns. Other flags that have special significance for sailors include the Blue Peter, the Yellow Jack, and the Jolly Roger.

BLUE PETER

This blue-and-white flag announces that a ship is ready to leave harbour.

YELLOW JACK

This bold ensign warns of fever on board. Other ships should steer clear.

JOLLY ROGER

The skull-and-crossbones emblem strikes fear into sailors, as it is the sign of a pirate ship.

Flag Writing

The semaphore system, in which the position of two flags represents the different letters of the alphabet, allows sailors to talk to one another when their ships are too far apart for voices to be heard.

A & 1 B & 2 C & 3 D & 4 E & 5 F & 6

G & 7 H & 8 I & 9 J & 0 & K L
"Letters follow"

M N O P Q R

S T U V W X

Y Z Numbers follow Error Attention

ACTIVITY: Can you read this message in semaphore?

CHAPTER 5

SIGNALLING AT NIGHT

Flags are useful only when they can be seen clearly. At night, sailors must rely on lights and sounds to convey important information. Morse code, which is central to the newly invented electrical telegraph system, can be used at sea to give long and short flashes of light from a hooded lantern.

LIGHTHOUSE

For a seafarer, there is no more welcome sight on a dark night than the beam of a lighthouse. In these buildings, a bright flame at the top of a tall tower is magnified through glass lenses to send a beam of light out to sea, warning ships of dangerous rocks.

FOGHORN

Even the brightest beam from a lighthouse can do little to penetrate dense fog. Along coastlines where fog is a common hazard, the authorities have built giant metal horns that are powered by compressed air. If you hear the deep note of a foghorn, steer away!

A sinking ship must attract the attention of anyone nearby. A gunpowder rocket flare combines a loud bang with a bright light, providing a very effective distress signal. Distress flares are much more powerful than ordinary firework rockets.

MORSE CODE

Invented by Samuel Morse in the 1830s, this code is used to send messages electronically. By tapping on a rocker switch, the operator can send a series of long and short electrical impulses representing letters of the alphabet through the telegraph cable.

A	.—	K	—.—	U	..—	4	....—
B	—...	L	.—..	V	...—	5	.....
C	—.—.	M	——	W	.——	6	—....
D	—..	N	—.	X	—..—	7	——...
E	.	O	———	Y	—.——	8	———..
F	..—.	P	.——.	Z	——..	9	————.
G	——.	Q	——.—	0	—————	Period	.—.—.—
H	....	R	.—.	1	.————	Comma	——..——
I	..	S	...	2	..———	Question Mark	..——..
J	.———	T	—	3	...——		

ACTIVITY: Can you spell out your name in Morse code?

Chapter 6
Ocean Hazards

Although ships are a fairly safe means of transport, it would be foolish to ignore the perils of ocean travel. As well as the hazard of treacherous rocks that could dash a ship to splinters, the greatest danger is that a huge wave might roll across the ocean surface, swamping the ship with water and dragging it down, along with its crew, to a final resting place on the seabed.

Shipwreck

A ship's hull may appear strong, but it is easily damaged, especially if burrowing sea worms have weakened its timbers. Submerged rocks and coral reefs, floating icebergs, or even collisions with other vessels can break through a hull and let the seawater flood in. If the damage is not too grave, the crew may have time to escape in lifeboats, although their chances of being picked up by another vessel are quite slim.

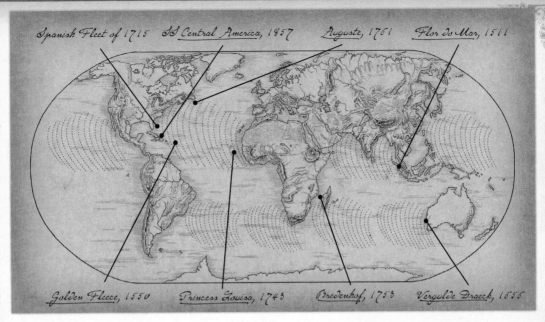

Spanish Fleet of 1715 SS Central America, 1857 Auguste, 1761 Flor do Mar, 1511

Golden Fleece, 1550 Princess Louisa, 1743 Bredenhof, 1753 Vergulde Draeck, 1656

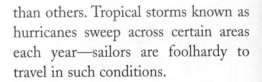

The pink lines indicate areas where tropical storms are most likely.
The black dots show the sites of several notable shipwrecks.

STORMY SEAS

In general, the number of shipwrecks increases with the amount of shipping along a particular route, but some parts of the ocean are much more dangerous than others. Tropical storms known as hurricanes sweep across certain areas each year—sailors are foolhardy to travel in such conditions.

BEASTS OF THE DEEP

The sudden, mysterious disappearance of ships at sea has long been attributed to the Leviathan or other supposed sea monsters. Modern science has found no evidence of giant sea serpents, but on this voyage we have witnessed first-hand the strength and size of the monstrous giant squid.

ACTIVITY: Can you find out what is meant by the "eye" of a hurricane?

CHAPTER 7

BENEATH THE WAVES

Since ancient times, people have dreamed of exploring the mysterious world beneath the ocean's surface. Until recently, however, this was an impossible dream. Would-be explorers not only had to solve the problem of breathing underwater but also had to find a way to protect themselves from the pressure of the water bearing down on them from above.

LEGENDARY VISIT

Among the many feats attributed by legend to the ancient Greek hero Alexander the Great was visiting the ocean depths. However, whilst Alexander did undoubtedly accomplish many great deeds, it can be confidently stated that deep-sea exploration was not one of them—the Ancient Greeks simply did not have the technology required to build a submarine.

WOODEN *TURTLE*

The world's first submarine was built in the newly declared United States in 1775 and took part in the Revolutionary War. David Bushnell's *Turtle* had a wooden, pear-shaped hull about 6 feet (2 metres) long. Carrying a single person, it could travel just below the surface powered by a hand-turned propeller, but it could not dive to any great depth.

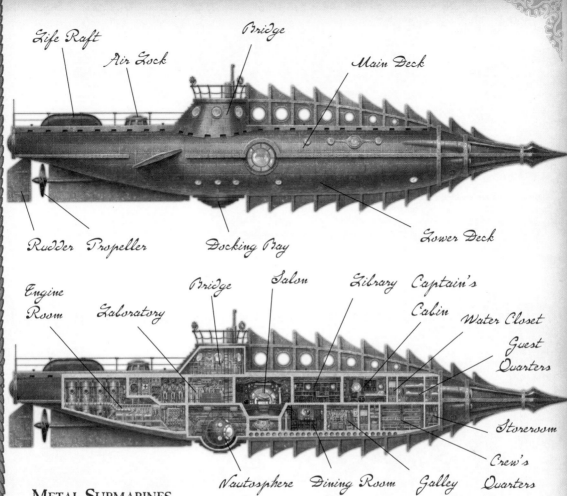

Life Raft — Bridge — Main Deck — Air Lock — Rudder — Propeller — Docking Bay — Lower Deck

Engine Room — Laboratory — Bridge — Salon — Library — Captain's Cabin — Water Closet — Guest Quarters — Nautosphere — Dining Room — Galley — Crew's Quarters — Storeroom

METAL SUBMARINES

During the present nineteenth century, there have been many advances in technology, such as the steam engine and the industrial manufacture of steel. Shipbuilders can now consider the construction of an undersea craft able to carry several passengers, and a certain Captain Nemo has already designed the steel-clad *Nautilus*, in which we are travelling today. We may be confident that such vessels will be fairly commonplace by the year 1900.

ACTIVITY: Water pressure increases by the equivalent of 1 atmosphere for every 10 metres. What is the pressure (in atmospheres) at a depth of 750 metres?

PUBLISHER'S NOTE
The *Nautilus* (pictured above), if it did indeed exist in 1863, was incredibly advanced for its time and should not be taken as an accurate representation of undersea vessels of the era.

CHAPTER 8

DIVING

A person can hold his or her breath underwater for only up to two or three minutes. However, the recent invention of the diving suit has allowed divers to spend much greater periods of time beneath the sea. Aboard the *Nautilus,* Captain Nemo's diving suits (pictured opposite) are far superior to any I have seen before, as they include their own air supply.

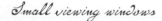

Small viewing windows

Air intake

Suit sealed above diver's knees and elbows

AN EARLY DIVING SUIT

In 1797 the German engineer Karl Klingert published his designs for a "diving machine" that consisted of an "open" metal helmet that rested on the diver's shoulders. Compressed air was pumped into the helmet from the surface. Klingert's innovative apparatus was reportedly tested in the Oder River, to the delight of the watching crowd.

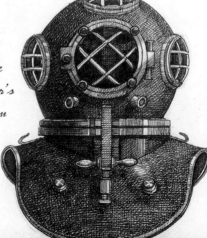

Modern "closed" diving helmets are sealed to the diver's suit and permit an all-round view.

BEWARE OF SHARKS

A diving suit will keep the water out, but it offers no protection against the razor-sharp teeth of a shark, which can appear from the gloom at any moment. Divers are advised to work in pairs so that one of them can keep a lookout for sharks and other dangers.

THE AIR LOCK

To prevent the *Nautilus* from flooding with water every time divers enter and exit the craft, an airtight compartment called an air lock is used. The technical advancements aboard this vessel never cease to amaze me.

Inside the submarine, a diver enters the air lock and seals the door.

The diver opens a valve to let seawater flow into the air lock.

When the air lock is flooded, the diver opens the upper door.

ACTIVITY: Draw and label your own design for a diving suit or a submarine. What features would you include, and why?

Chapter 9

Sunken Treasure

Whilst the pursuit of scientific knowledge should be the main purpose of undersea exploration, there are other reasons to venture beneath the waves. Hundreds, if not thousands, of shipwrecks litter the ocean floor. Some of these wrecks once carried valuable cargoes that can be salvaged, and a few of them contain strongboxes filled with treasure.

Gold and Jewels

In the days before banknotes and chequebooks, people had to carry their wealth in the form of precious metals and gems. Sometimes, entire ships were filled with gold and silver to transport across the oceans. These treasure ships were often so heavily laden that they could only just stay afloat in calm weather. Even a moderate storm was enough to capsize a vessel and send it plunging to the ocean floor.

Many metals rust and become discoloured when they are immersed in seawater, but gold remains bright and untarnished.

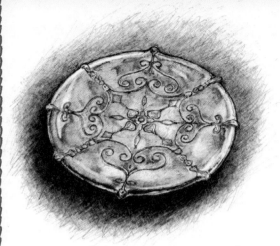

A silver plate salvaged from a shipwreck

FINDERS, KEEPERS

According to the ancient and unwritten laws of the sea, the cargo and valuables aboard a wrecked ship belong to whoever salvages them. If a ship is wrecked in shallow water, its owner may be able to send divers down to reclaim the goods. In deeper water, however, this may be impossible, so the wreck and its treasure will remain undisturbed for centuries.

RECOVERED KNOWLEDGE

Even if a wrecked ship contains no gold or jewels, it may still be a treasure trove of information. By studying the items recovered from a wreck, ocean explorers can learn a great deal about the people who sailed in that ship. The weapons, armour, drinking cups, eating implements, and kitchen utensils all provide clues as to where and when the ship was built and who was aboard when it sank.

An eighteenth-century military helmet salvaged from the wreck of the French ship Astrolabe, which sank in 1788. The metal crest may once have held a plume of feathers.

ACTIVITY: Can you explain why metal and pottery items such as weapons, armour, drinking cups, and kitchen utensils are often found in shipwrecks, whereas books, feathers, clothing, and bed linen are very rarely recovered?

Chapter 10

Myths of the Sea

The dark and mysterious depths have given rise to countless myths and legends concerning sea monsters, merfolk, and drowned cities. Proper scientific investigation and the constant progress of knowledge will no doubt reveal what, if any, truth there is behind these outlandish tales.

Sea Monsters

There is a widespread and enduring myth that the ocean contains huge monsters—the Leviathan, Scylla, and the kraken, to name but a few—that occasionally rise from the depths to drag ships to their doom. Whilst it is true that the oceans are home to whales, which are the largest animals on Earth, these slow and non-aggressive creatures pose no threat to any seaworthy vessel. Little is yet known about the nature of the giant squid, but in the course of my research, I aim to uncover more.

Merfolk

Many sailors believe that merfolk— humans with fishes' tails—live beneath the waves. In the absence of any proof as to the existence of these creatures, it seems wise to assume that tales of merfolk are based upon sightings of seals or sea cows (manatees).

ATLANTIS

According to an ancient Greek myth, Atlantis was a marvellous and highly civilised island city ruled over by the sea god Poseidon. The island was said to have sunk suddenly beneath the waves, leaving no trace. The Greek philosopher Plato believed that Atlantis was located in the Atlantic Ocean beyond what he called the Pillars of Hercules, which we know today as the Strait of Gibraltar. Despite many attempts being made,

nobody has yet succeeded in locating this legendary lost city.*

* PUBLISHER'S NOTE
It appears from the journal of Zoticus de Lesseps (*Oceanology*) that the crew of the *Nautilus* did indeed succeed in discovering Atlantis, toward the end of their ill-fated voyage.

ACTIVITY: Some people believe that the legend of Atlantis is connected with the explosion of the volcano Thera in about 1600 BC. Can you find out the modern name of the island where this volcano was located?

CHAPTER 11

OCEAN EXPLORERS

The Age of Exploration began in 1492 when Christopher Columbus crossed the Atlantic and discovered America. Other voyages and discoveries soon followed. For example, Vasco da Gama crossed the Indian Ocean in 1498 and returned to Portugal as a hero. However, exploring the oceans is a dangerous enterprise, as Magellan, Cook, and many others all found to their cost.

MAGELLAN EMBARKS

Ferdinand Magellan (shown right) was a Portuguese navigator employed by Spain. In 1519 he led a small fleet of ships across the Atlantic, around the tip of South America, and into an unknown ocean that he named the Pacific (meaning "peaceful"). Supplies ran so low that the crews suffered great hardships and were even reduced to eating their own shoes.

KILLED IN BATTLE

Eventually the fleet reached the island of Cebu in Indonesia, where they received a warm welcome from the islanders. Magellan was persuaded to help the natives in a war against a neighbouring island. During one of the ensuing battles, Magellan was killed, along with many of his sailors.

AROUND THE WORLD

The survivors escaped in the *Victoria*, under the command of Juan Sebastián Elcano. The *Victoria* sailed around Africa and back into the Atlantic. In 1522, after nearly three years at sea, she returned to Spain, having completed the first round-the-world voyage.

CAPTAIN COOK

James Cook was sent by the British
government to carry out astronomical
observations on the Pacific island of Tahiti.
He was also given secret instructions to
search for the rumoured Southern Continent
(Australasia). During 1769–1770, Cook
made a detailed survey of New Zealand and
the eastern coast of Australia. On a later
voyage he discovered the Hawaiian Islands,
where he was killed in 1779 during an
argument with a native chieftain.

*Captain Cook (1728–1779) is credited with
discovering Australia, although other navigators
had previously sighted stretches of its coastline.*

COOK'S VOYAGES

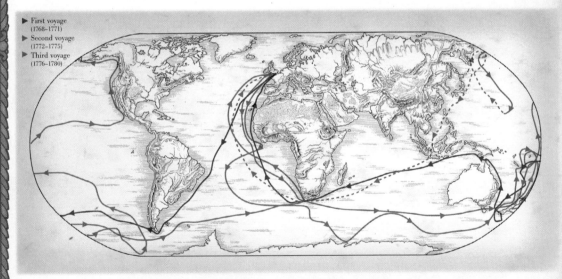

► First voyage
(1768–1771)
► Second voyage
(1772–1775)
► Third voyage
(1776–1780)

*On his first voyage, Cook travelled to Tahiti, New Zealand, and Australia; on the
second voyage, he circumnavigated Antarctica; and on the third voyage he met his death
in the Hawaiian Islands. The route of the surviving crew is shown in blue dots.*

ACTIVITY: Can you find out the names of the four ships used by Captain Cook during
his voyages of exploration?

Chapter 12

The Fate of La Pérouse

In 1785 the French explorer Jean-François de Galaup, Comte de La Pérouse, set out on a round-the-world voyage with two ships: the *Boussole* and the *Astrolabe*. He explored the coasts of California and Alaska as well as the Hawaiian Islands. In 1788 La Pérouse briefly visited Australia. However, after departing from Australia, neither of his two ships was ever seen again.

Shipwreck and Massacre

Fragments of wreckage subsequently recovered from the shorelines of the Santa Cruz Islands have provided clues as to the fate of La Pérouse's expedition. Both ships are believed to have been wrecked on a coral reef, and hostile islanders are thought to have killed many of the crew. The survivors built a raft from the timbers of the *Astrolabe*, only to vanish without trace in the vast Pacific.

The Astrolabe was about 130 feet (40 metres) long and carried a crew of ten officers and one hundred sailors.

TRADING GOODS

The *Boussole* carried casks of coloured glass beads that the crew hoped to trade with the natives. Hundreds of these beads were scattered across the reef when the ship was wrecked.

SHIP'S BELL

The *Astrolabe*'s bronze bell, already encrusted with marine growth, was discovered in 1827 by the Irish sea captain Peter Dillon.

LOUIS D'OR

This French gold coin, found off the islands of Santa Cruz, bears the portrait of King Louis XVI, who appointed La Pérouse to command the expedition. The king hoped that La Pérouse's discoveries would rival Captain Cook's.

ACTIVITY: Can you find out how King Louis XVI of France lost his head?

Oceanologists have many tools at their disposal to help them in their understanding of the world's waters.

PART 2

UNDERSTANDING THE OCEANS

The second section of this handbook is intended to inform the reader as to the constantly changing nature of the oceans. The Earth's bodies of water are in a state of perpetual motion, driven by winds, currents, and tides. Furthermore, as I shall reveal, the supposedly solid surface of our planet itself is also shifting—usually very slowly, but sometimes with the sudden shock of an earthquake.

The changing surface of the Earth has caused some ancient cities to sink beneath the sea. Their streets can now be trodden only by those who are properly equipped for underwater exploration.

Chapter 13

Light and Depth

Beneath the surface, the oceans extend to depths of more than 6 miles (10 kilometres). Sunlight can penetrate only the first few hundred feet, so most of the ocean is in permanent darkness.

Depth Zones

- ✳ Surface Zone: 0–30 feet (0–10 metres)
- ✳ Sunlit Zone: 30–660 feet (10–200 metres)
- ✳ Twilight Zone: 660–3,300 feet (200–1,000 metres)

- ✳ Midnight Zone: 3,300–13,000 feet (1,000–4,000 metres)
- ✳ The Abyss: 13,000–20,000 feet (4,000–6,000 metres)
- ✳ The Trenches: below 20,000 feet (6,000 metres)

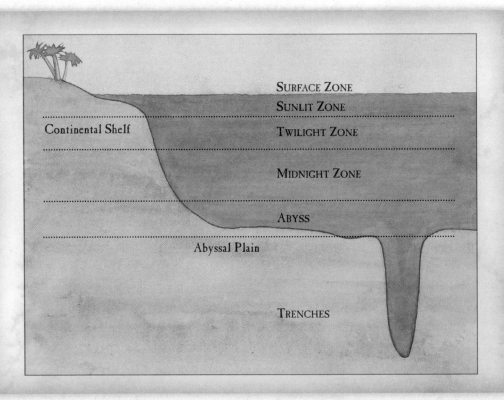

Surface Zone

Sunlit Zone

Continental Shelf

Twilight Zone

Midnight Zone

Abyss

Abyssal Plain

Trenches

OCEAN FEATURE	LOCATION	DEPTH
EURASIAN BASIN	North of the Bering Strait in the Arctic Ocean	3 ⅓ miles (5.4 kilometres)
SOUTH SANDWICH TRENCH	In the Weddell Sea in the Southern Ocean	4 ½ miles (7.2 kilometres)
JAVA TRENCH	Off the coast of Sumatra in the Indian Ocean	4 ⅔ miles (7.5 kilometres)
PUERTO RICO TRENCH	Off the coast of Florida in the Atlantic Ocean	5 ¾ miles (9.2 kilometres)
MARIANA TRENCH	Near the Mariana Islands in the Pacific Ocean	6 ¾ miles (10.9 kilometres)

OCEAN TRENCHES

Out in the middle of the ocean, where the average depth of water is about 3 miles (5 kilometres), the seabed is mainly a flat and featureless plain covered with thick mud. In various locations, however, the ocean floor suddenly plunges away into a narrow trench that can be more than twice that depth. These deep trenches, which were presumably formed by earthquakes, are the lowest points on the planet's surface.

LIGHTING THE DARKNESS

Despite the absence of sunlight, the deeper parts of the ocean are not totally without light. Many species of deep-sea fish have the ability to produce their own illumination. The anglerfish, for example, has a glowing lure that dangles in front of its mouth to attract prey.

ACTIVITY: Depth of water is often measured in fathoms. Can you find out the depth (in feet and metres) of 10 fathoms?

CHAPTER 14

WIND AND WAVES

The ocean's surface is rarely still and smooth like a millpond. It is usually in a state of constant up-and-down motion. This is caused by the wind. When the wind blows over the sea, it transfers some of its energy to the surface water. This energy travels across the ocean in the form of waves—the stronger the wind, the bigger the waves.

WIND

Wind is not caused by supernatural beings blowing out their breath; it is the result of the air being heated by the sun. Some parts of the Earth receive more heat than others, so the air there is warmer. This warmer air weighs less than cooler air, so it rises. Cool air then moves in to replace the rising warm air. This flow of air is what we call the wind.

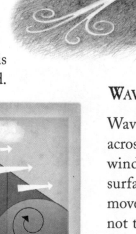

WAVES

Waves are energy moving across the ocean, caused by the wind dragging across the surface. The surface water moves in small circles but does not travel very far. You can see this if you watch a float bobbing in the waves—it moves up and down but does not travel horizontally. The energy is transferred across the surface, causing these circular motions along the way.

Shake a rope and you will see ripples pass along it, just as waves pass across the ocean.

WIND BELTS

Although the direction and strength of the wind is difficult to predict from one day to the next, there is an overall pattern to the way the winds move around the world. The sun's heat produces a constant flow of air from the warm tropics to the much cooler poles and back. This circulation of air is separated into a series of wind belts because the Earth is rotating.

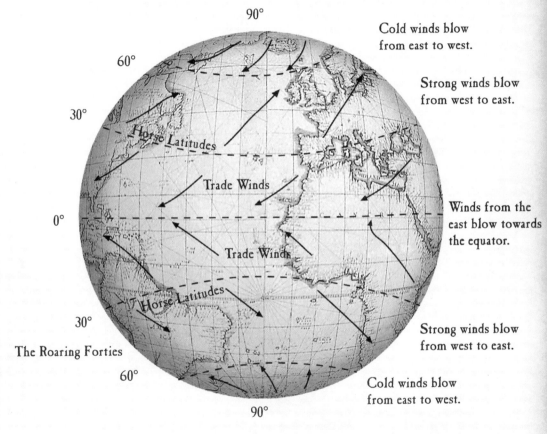

90°

60°

30°

Horse Latitudes

Trade Winds

0°

Trade Winds

Horse Latitudes

30°

The Roaring Forties

60°

90°

Cold winds blow from east to west.

Strong winds blow from west to east.

Winds from the east blow towards the equator.

Strong winds blow from west to east.

Cold winds blow from east to west.

Through the ages, sailors have given names to regions with distinctive wind patterns. The "Roaring Forties" is the region around forty degrees south of the equator with reliably strong winds.

In the "Horse Latitudes," the winds are very light, so sailing ships were often becalmed. Legend has it that sailors were forced to throw their horses overboard to preserve water.

ACTIVITY: How did the trade winds get their name?

CHAPTER 15

CURRENTS

Waves are a temporary disturbance of the ocean's surface, but the winds also affect the ocean in more substantial ways. They can create surface currents—flows of water on the surface. These currents move like endless rivers in great loops around the ocean.

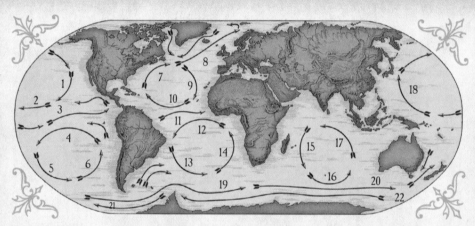

SURFACE CURRENTS

1. California Current
2. North Equatorial Current
3. Equatorial Counter Current
4. South Equatorial Current
5. South Pacific Current
6. Peruvian Current
7. Gulf Stream
8. North Atlantic Current
9. Canary Current
10. North Equatorial Current
11. Equatorial Counter Current
12. South Equatorial Current
13. Brazil Current
14. Benguela Current
15. Mozambique Current
16. South Indian Current
17. West Australian Current
18. North Pacific Current
19 & 20. West Wind Drift
21 & 22. East Wind Drift

SURFACE CURRENTS

In the same way that the wind belts circulate air around the planet, the wind-driven surface currents move water around the world. Generally, the currents that flow away from the equator carry warm water, while those that flow towards the equator carry cooler water.

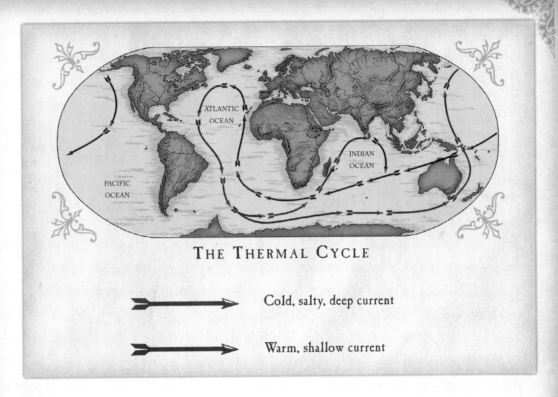

THE THERMAL CYCLE

→ Cold, salty, deep current

→ Warm, shallow current

DEEP CURRENTS

Deep below the ocean's surface, there is a different type of circulation that is driven by cold water from the poles. There, when seawater freezes, the salt in it does not freeze, so a lot of cold, very salty water is left. It is heavier than the surrounding water, so it sinks to the bottom in the polar regions. Then, warmer, lighter water moves in to take its place. The descending cold water drives a vast current of slightly warmer and less salty water through the Pacific, Indian, and Atlantic Oceans.*

ACTIVITY: Cold water sinks to the bottom, so why does frozen water float?

*PUBLISHER'S NOTE
The cycle described here was not widely known about at the time Aronnax was supposedly writing. The scientists on board the *Nautilus* seem most insightful and ahead of their time.

CHAPTER 16

TIDES AND COASTS

In open water, sailors have only to reckon with the effects of winds and currents. Near coastlines, however, they must also pay attention to the tide: the daily rise and fall in sea level. The difference between high and low tide varies considerably, depending on the shape of the coastline.

GRAVITY'S PULL

The tide is caused by the pull of the moon's gravity on the huge mass of water in the world's oceans. This pull creates a bulge of water on the side of the Earth closest to the moon. There is also a bulge on the side farthest from the moon, because the moon is "pulling the Earth away" from the water on that side, as it were. Because the Earth rotates once daily, there will be two high tides on any coastline every day (once when the area is on the side closest to the moon, and once when it is farthest away).

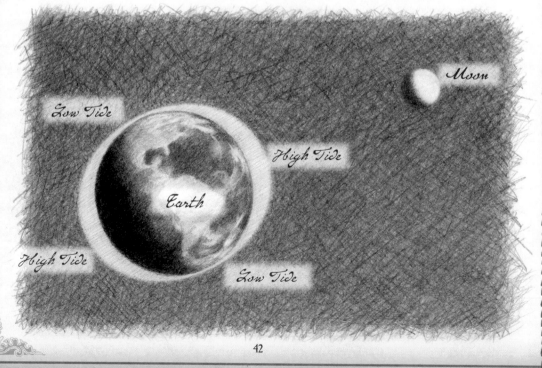

BEACHES

A beach is a sloping piece of coastline. At high tide, a beach is beneath the water, but at low tide it is part of the land. Beaches are covered with sand or pebbles that have been washed up by the waves. On beaches with a gentle slope, the horizontal distance between the points of high and low tide can be more than ⅔ mile (1 kilometre).

The structures shown below are called stacks. They are created by the actions of waves and tides.

CLIFFS

Cliffs are a more abrupt boundary between land and sea and are found along rocky coastlines. Waves can eventually wear away even the hardest rock. As the water removes the rock along the waterline, the rocks above are no longer supported, so they collapse to form sheer walls that can tower nearly 1,000 feet (300 metres) above the surface.

ACTIVITY: In some places, such as the Mediterranean coastline, the tidal range (the difference between high and low tides) is quite small. Can you find out where in the world the biggest tidal range occurs?

Chapter 17

The Ocean Floor

The oceanic depths are mysterious and remote. They are incredibly challenging to explore because of the difficulties of designing safe equipment. Aboard the *Nautilus* we are the fortunate few who are able to travel beneath the waves, yet most scientists must content themselves with the scraps of information that can be dredged up from the ocean floor.

Underwater Mountains

In addition to trenches (see page 37), the ocean floor also features mountains. The tallest peaks rise above the surface, their summits making islands, such as the Hawaiian Islands and the Azores.

The tallest mountain on Earth is largely underwater. It is Mauna Kea, in Hawaii. Underwater mountains whose summits are just below the surface are known as seamounts, or guyots.

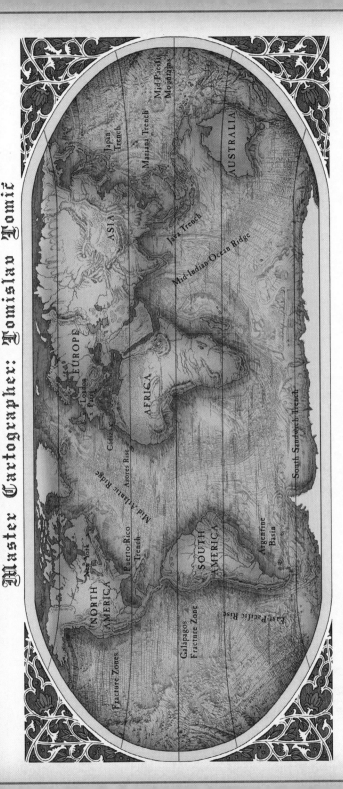

MAPPING THE SEABED

Measuring the depth of the ocean is a challenging and time-consuming process. In order to get an accurate measurement, a ship must be completely still in the water. A long, weighted line is dropped over the side and allowed to sink until it reaches the seabed. The line is measured as it is hauled back aboard, and the depth is recorded. By carefully plotting the position of hundreds of depth measurements, marine scientists are able to produce maps of the ocean floor.

Chapter 18

A Shifting Surface

For a better understanding of the oceans, it is necessary to consider the Earth as a whole. It seems likely that our planet's solid surface is not a single continuous layer but is divided into a number of separate plates.*

Constant Movement

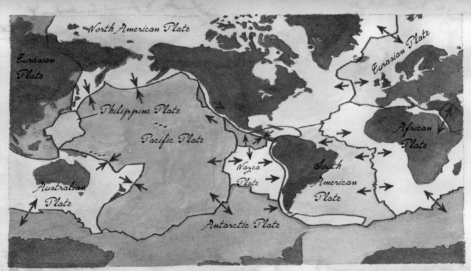

The Moving Plates of the Earth's Surface

These surface plates are locked together like the pieces of a gigantic jigsaw puzzle, and they move very slowly in different directions. The plates float on the molten rock of the Earth's interior and are dragged around by vast thermal currents beneath the surface. This movement of the surface plates is extremely slow—less than ⅓ inch (1 centimetre) per year in some cases—but it can have enormous effects on the shape of the land and the seabed, especially along the boundaries between plates.

* PUBLISHER'S NOTE
Despite an increasing amount of evidence, the scientific community resisted the idea of a shifting surface until the 1960s, when the theory of plate tectonics became generally accepted.

Close Continents

The close fit in shape between the east coast of South America and the west coast of Africa suggests that the Earth's landmasses were once joined and have since moved apart due to the shifting plates. The fact that the same types of rock and fossil can be found on opposite sides of the Atlantic Ocean, for example, in Scotland and Canada, supports this idea.

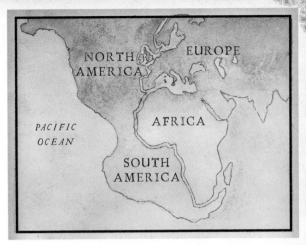

This map shows how the vast continents of our Earth may once have fitted together.

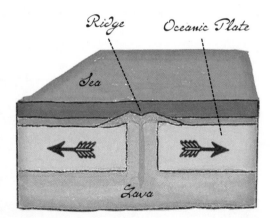

Constructive Boundary

Where two plates are moving apart, molten rock flows up from the Earth's interior to fill the gap. This area is called a constructive boundary, because the planet's solid surface is being "constructed." Constructive boundaries are usually found beneath the ocean.

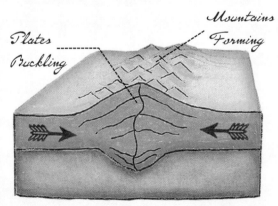

Collision Boundary

Where two plates meet in a head-on collision, the tremendous force that results from this collision makes the rocks bulge and buckle upwards, forming massive mountain ranges.

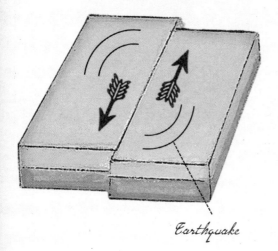

Continental Plates

Earthquake

CONSERVATIVE BOUNDARY

Where two plates slide past each other, the Earth's surface is neither deformed nor destroyed. This area is called a conservative boundary, because the existing surface is conserved. However, earthquakes can occur in these regions when the plates lock together then give way suddenly, releasing an enormous force that shakes the ground.

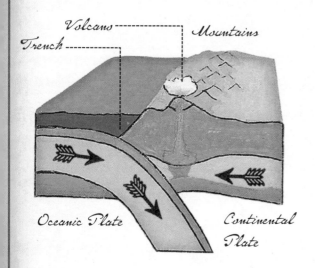

Volcano

Trench

Mountains

Oceanic Plate

Continental Plate

DESTRUCTIVE BOUNDARY

This type of boundary occurs when one plate is pushed beneath another. The solid surface of the lower plate melts because of the heat of the Earth's interior. Molten rock can be forced up to the surface, resulting in volcanic eruptions. The edge of the upper plate can be forced upwards to form mountains, and the surface is unstable. Earthquakes, as well as volcanoes, are common along these types of boundaries.

* PUBLISHER'S NOTE
This type of wave is now known as a tsunami.
The word is derived from the Japanese words *tsu*,
meaning "harbour," and *nami*, meaning "wave."
The word was first used in 1897.

DEADLY WAVES

Underwater earthquakes often cause huge waves, which travel at high speed across the ocean's surface. In mid-ocean, one such wave may be only about 3 feet (1 metre) high, but when it reaches shallow water along a coast, it becomes an onrushing wall of water up to 70 feet (20 metres) tall.*

VOLCANOES

A volcano occurs when molten rock from the Earth's interior finds its way to the surface. Layers of molten rock solidify over time to form a distinctive cone-shaped mountain. In some cases the outflow of molten rock is slow and steady, but in other cases it may be violently explosive and accompanied by vast amounts of gas and ash. Volcanoes appear both on land and underwater.

ACTIVITY: Can you find out the name of your nearest active volcano?

CHAPTER 19

UNDERSEA CABLES

The scientific exploration of the ocean floor has paved the way for what is perhaps the greatest technological advance of the nineteenth century. An undersea telegraph cable now carries messages instantly across the Atlantic Ocean between the continents of Europe and North America. In the future, a network of such cables will connect every corner of the globe.

THE FIRST OCEANOLOGIST

Matthew Maury (born in 1806) may rightfully be considered the first modern oceanologist. He began his career as an officer in the United States Navy but was forced to take a desk job after being injured in a stagecoach accident. He was appointed head of the Navy's Depot of Charts and Instruments, where he began gathering information on ocean winds and currents. He also made a special study of the Atlantic seabed.

AN OCEANOLOGIST'S BIBLE

In 1855, Maury published his findings in *The Physical Geography of the Sea*—the first comprehensive book that covered all aspects of the oceans. In particular, his detailed descriptions of the physical contours of the seabed were crucial in persuading people that a transatlantic telegraph cable was indeed feasible.

THE TRANSATLANTIC TELEGRAPH CABLE

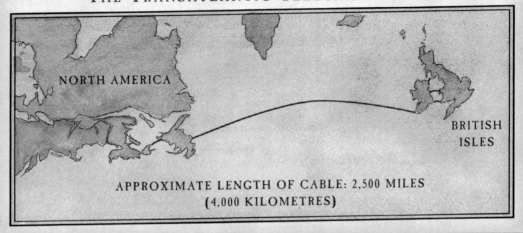

NORTH AMERICA

BRITISH ISLES

APPROXIMATE LENGTH OF CABLE: 2,500 MILES
(4,000 KILOMETRES)

THE TRANSATLANTIC TELEGRAPH

The electric telegraph, which was invented in 1832 (see page 19), has rapidly become one of the essential features of modern life. People in Europe and North America have become accustomed to exchanging messages with distant cities, to the great advancement of trade and commerce. Since 1858, a single cable that runs for some 2,500 miles (4,000 kilometres) beneath the Atlantic has linked the two continents.

ARMOURED CABLE

Overland telegraph cables consist of a single strand of copper wire stretched between upright posts. If the cables break, they are easily repaired. Breaks in undersea cables, however, are much more difficult to repair, so a multi-stranded copper cable is used. The copper cable is wrapped in waterproof insulation and is further protected by an outer coating of iron wires.

ACTIVITY: On August 16, 1858, Queen Victoria sent the first transatlantic telegram to President Buchanan of the United States. Can you find out what it said? What would you have written?

Surface Zone

Sunlit Zone

Twilight Zone

Midnight Zone

The Abyss

The Trenches

Each level of the ocean has its own community of sea creatures, although the number of different species tends to decrease the deeper you go.

PART 3

LIFE IN THE OCEANS

The final part of our course will introduce the reader to the living oceans. In this section, we will meet the wonderful variety of plants and animals that dwell beneath the waves. I shall demonstrate how all these countless species, many of which inhabit very different environments—from sunlit waters to inky depths—are linked in a web of life that extends far beyond the ocean to include all living creatures on the planet.

I never believed I would set eyes on a giant squid, but this voyage has revealed wonders far beyond the limits of my imagination.

CHAPTER 20

ANIMALS OF THE SEA

All of Earth's creatures can be arranged into a series of groups and subgroups. Animals that have similar physical characteristics are grouped together. For example, all animals with a backbone (called vertebrates) are placed in the group *Chordata*—a Latin word meaning "corded"—as they all have a spinal cord. The web of life below shows the different groups into which ocean and coast-dwelling animals can be divided.

> **Activity:** Species are identified by a two-part Latin name: the blue whale, for example, is *Balaenoptera musculus*. The first name establishes the "genus" (a type of subgroup) that a creature belongs to, and the second name identifies the particular species. Can you find out who devised this naming system (which is called the binomial system)?

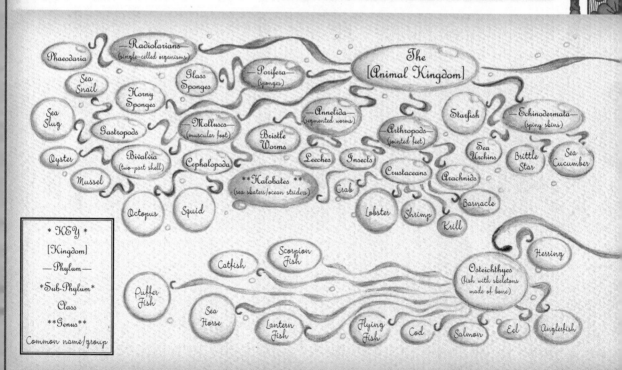

OCEAN DRIFTERS

All land animals have the power of locomotion, which means they can move about using their muscles. In the ocean, however, this is unnecessary, because water makes creatures float. Many smaller sea animals, such as the radiolarian shown on the left, spend their lives drifting weightlessly, carried along by the ocean currents.

BLUE GIANT

Whales are by far the largest animals on the planet. They have been able to grow much larger than land animals because the water helps support their weight. The biggest of the whales, the blue whale, measures some 100 feet (30 metres) in length when fully grown.

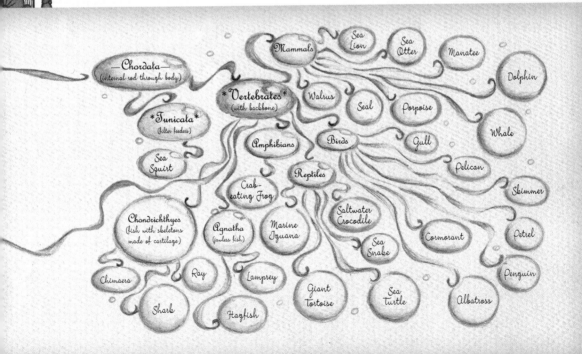

Chordata
(internal rod through body)

Tunicata
(filter feeders)

Vertebrates
(with backbone)

Mammals

Sea Lion

Sea Otter

Manatee

Dolphin

Walrus

Seal

Porpoise

Whale

Sea Squirt

Amphibians

Birds

Gull

Pelican

Reptiles

Skimmer

Crab-eating Frog

Chondrichthyes
(fish with skeletons made of cartilage)

Agnatha
(jawless fish)

Marine Iguana

Saltwater Crocodile

Sea Snake

Cormorant

Petrel

Chimaera

Ray

Lamprey

Giant Tortoise

Sea Turtle

Albatross

Penguin

Shark

Hagfish

CHAPTER 21

BEAKS AND BONES

The largest animals in the sea are vertebrates (creatures with a backbone). Animals from all the main vertebrate groups live in the oceans, apart from amphibians (the group that includes frogs and salamanders). This is because delicate amphibian skin cannot cope with the saltiness of seawater.

WHALES AND DOLPHINS

Whales and dolphins are ocean-dwelling mammals that look rather like fish. They breathe air from the surface and are warm-blooded (which means they can keep their temperature constant). Fish, however, extract oxygen from water through their gills and are cold-blooded (their temperature depends on their surroundings).

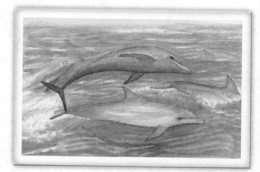

FURRY MAMMALS

Seals, sea lions, and walruses are marine mammals with whiskers and furry bodies. Although these animals spend most of their time in the sea, they clamber onto land to sleep and give birth to their pups.

BIRDS

Although most seabirds gather around coastlines, some, such as the albatross, fly right across the oceans. The albatross is one of the largest birds in the world, with a wingspan close to 9 feet (3 metres).

Reptiles

There are only a small number of reptiles in the oceans: a few species of sea snakes and sea turtles, and just one species of sea lizard—the marine iguana of the Galápagos Islands in the eastern Pacific. These iguanas dive off rocks to feed on seaweed at depths of up to 16 feet (5 metres).

Fish

There are two main groups of fish: those with skeletons made of bone and those with skeletons made of cartilage. The majority of fish fall into the first category. Shiny scales cover their bodies, and their fins are thin and semi-transparent, with visible stiffening rods radiating outwards.

Flying fish
(Exocoetus volitans)

Sharks and Rays

Sharks, and their relatives the rays and chimaeras, are the only vertebrates whose skeletons are made of soft cartilage rather than hard bone. Instead of scales, they have tiny plates embedded in their skin, giving them a smooth outline to help them glide along.

Blue-spotted stingray
(Taeniura lymma)

ACTIVITY: Try to guess how many different shark species there are—then do some research to find out whether you were right.

CHAPTER 22

BONELESS BEASTS

The marine invertebrates are sea creatures without a backbone. This group is wonderfully varied, including animals of many shapes and sizes. Some of them, such as the jellyfish, lack any form of skeleton. Others, such as the crustaceans (crabs, shrimps, and lobsters), have an outer skeleton similar to that of insects.

SIMPLE ANIMALS

Jellyfish, sea anemones, and other such creatures are sometimes called "simple animals" because they do not have arms or legs. A jellyfish is, however, an extremely well-designed animal. It is able to swim by rhythmically contracting its muscles, and each trailing tentacle carries a venomous sting at its tip for killing prey or for defence against other hunters.

TENTACLED TERRORS

The octopus, squid, and cuttlefish belong to a group of molluscs called the cephalopods. Their soft bodies have long, flexible tentacles, which they use to seize prey and drag it to their mouths. The largest known octopus is only about 14 feet (4 metres) long, yet on our voyage we have witnessed a giant squid that measured 60 feet (18 metres) from end to end!

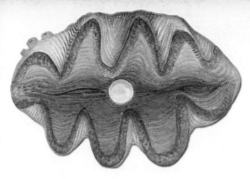

MOLLUSCS

The two largest groups of molluscs are the bivalves and the gastropods. Bivalves, including the clam, shown left, have two matching shells that cover the body when they are closed. Most gastropods, such as the snail, have a single spiral shell that the animal can retreat into. Some—for instance, the slug—do not have a shell at all.

CRABS

Crabs can survive out of water for long periods of time, so they live along the seashore as well as on the seabed. Some crab species live mainly on land and have even been known to climb trees.

SHRIMP

Shrimp are often found in large numbers in areas with a sandy seabed. Most shrimp are small and have transparent bodies, so they can be difficult to see in the water.

LOBSTERS

These clawed beasts, like crabs and shrimp, belong to a group of crustaceans known as the decapods, because they have ten legs (the Latin word *decem* means "ten"). A lobster's front legs have a pair of powerful pincers for tearing apart food.

ACTIVITY: What is the name of the group that includes insects and crustaceans?

CHAPTER 23

MARINE PLANTS

Plants in the ocean live on or near the surface and are categorised according to their colour. Green seaweed grows in shallow water, brown seaweed grows in deeper water, and red seaweed is able to grow in the deepest water of all three.

SEAWEED

Seaweed is a type of algae—a group of plant-like organisms that don't have roots and usually live in water. Seaweeds attach themselves to a rock or the seafloor by a tough anchor called a holdfast. This prevents them from being carried away by the current. Some holdfasts stay in place for forty years, producing more and more seaweed. The feathery fronds of seaweed do the same job as leaves on a land plant: they convert sunlight into food.

Red: *Palmaria palmata*   Green: *Caulerpa flexilis*   Brown: *Saccharina latissima*

KELP FORESTS

Kelp, a type of brown seaweed, is the largest kind of algae. Individual kelp plants can reach a height of 100 feet (30 metres). These grow in offshore waters and often form dense "forests" on the sandy seabed. Such kelp forests attract a wide variety of marine life.

WEEDY WONDER

One species of fish has developed the most incredible camouflage. The weedy sea dragon, which is related to the sea horse, has a number of strangely shaped fleshy lobes dangling from its body. When the creature hides among seaweed, these lobes look like wafting seaweed fronds, keeping it hidden.

ACTIVITY: Draw an underwater scene with the three types of seaweed—red, green, and brown—at different depths. Include some fish and other marine creatures hiding in the seaweed.

CHAPTER 24

A FOOD WEB

The most important plants in the sea are the smallest ones. Near the sunlit surface, every bucket of water contains many thousands of microscopic algae. These algae are food for the ocean's tiny, drifting animals, and together these minuscule plants and animals form the basis of the ocean's food web.

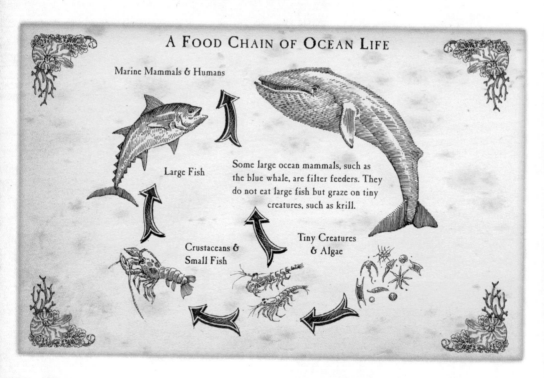

A FOOD CHAIN OF OCEAN LIFE

Marine Mammals & Humans

Large Fish

Some large ocean mammals, such as the blue whale, are filter feeders. They do not eat large fish but graze on tiny creatures, such as krill.

Crustaceans & Small Fish

Tiny Creatures & Algae

THE WEB OF LIFE

Every living thing in the ocean is part of an enormous food web that is made up of countless food chains. In one such chain (shown on the left of the diagram above), tiny creatures and algae are eaten by krill, which are eaten by a lobster, which is eaten by a fish. In another much shorter chain (above right), the smaller creatures are eaten directly by a large whale.

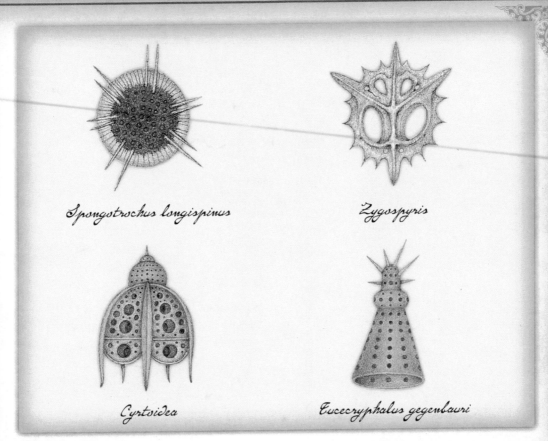

Spongotrochus longispinus

Zygospyris

Cyrtoidea

Eucecryphalus gegenbauri

RADIOLARIANS

Whilst the ocean's larger animals are by now fairly well known to science, we are constantly making new and exciting discoveries about the sea's microscopic creatures. Many of these tiny creatures are, in fact, immature forms of larger animals, which will eventually grow to become fish or crustaceans, for example. Others, however, remain a diminutive size throughout their lives. Professor Haeckel has recently made a detailed study of one such group: the radiolarians. Less than a millimetre in diameter, these minute animals are made of a single cell. Their bodies are supported by an intricately shaped mineral skeleton, each species with its own distinctive shape. The buildup of radiolarian skeletons on the seabed is one of the main components of the mud that covers the deep ocean floor.

ACTIVITY: Fresh water also contains tiny plants and animals. Collect some water from a pond (or from a tide pool, if you live near the coast) and examine it using a powerful magnifying glass (or under a microscope). Make drawings of anything that you can see.

Chapter 25

The Upper Ocean

The ocean can be divided into different zones, depending on depth (see page 36). The upper zones of the ocean are by far the most densely populated with animal life. Sunlight warms the shallow waters, causing plant life to thrive, which attracts animals that feed on these plants. These animals in turn attract many larger predators.

1. Common Gull
2. Albatross
3. Common Dolphin
4. Humpback Whale
5. Arctic Tern
6. Crab

The surface zone is the realm of creatures that breathe air: both seabirds that swoop down to pluck food from the water and mammals that rise to the surface every so often to fill their lungs. The surface zone is also the home of shore-dwelling creatures, such as gulls and crabs.

SUNLIT ZONE

1. Coral
2. Reef Fish
3. Tuna
4. Manta Ray
5. Great White Shark
6. Jellyfish

Just beneath the surface, the sunlit zone teems with life. Predators of every shape and size are attracted by the abundance of food in this sunlit zone. A particular feature of waters at this depth in tropical regions is the presence of coral reefs. They are found where the water is less than 230 feet (70 metres) deep. These reefs contain the greatest number and variety of animal species to be found anywhere in the oceans.

EMPEROR ANGELFISH

The striking emperor angelfish is found in coral reefs throughout the Indian and Pacific Oceans. The young have circular blue and white makings, while the adults have blue and yellow stripes (as shown at left). These fish can crush shrimp and shellfish between their powerful jaws.

ACTIVITY: Can you find out which is the largest coral reef in the world? Try sketching some pictures of creatures that live there.

Chapter 26

Coral Reefs

Until quite recently, coral was considered to be a strange, slow-growing marine plant. In fact, however, a piece of coral is a colony of tiny animals that are related to jellyfish. These animals construct stony outer skeletons to protect and support their bodies. Each generation builds upon the skeletons of previous generations, and over time a reef is created.

Fringing Reef

A fringing reef is one that grows directly from the shore. When a volcano's cone thrusts itself above the surface, it creates a region of shallow water around it where coral can flourish. The coral gradually builds up to form a fringing reef.

Barrier Reef

A barrier reef is one separated from the land by a deep lagoon. Over time, islands such as the one shown here may sink back under the sea or become worn away by waves. The coral continues to grow, forming a barrier around the remains of the land. Sand sometimes builds up on top of the reef, and plants may take root.

Atoll

Long after the island has vanished beneath the waves, evidence of its former existence remains in the form of an atoll—an almost circular ring of coral surrounding a lagoon.

Brain Coral

This intriguing-looking coral is called brain coral, because it forms a rounded, wrinkled structure that very much resembles the labyrinthine surface of the human brain.

Orange Tree Coral

Some coral imitates the branching shapes of trees. Each branch is covered with hundreds of coral creatures that snatch tiny drifting animals to eat from the water with their tentacles.

Elkhorn Coral

This species of coral grows to mimic another natural structure—that of the flattened antlers of an elk.

Fire Coral

Fire coral is to be treated with caution and should on no account be touched with bare skin. The animals of this coral species are equipped with a venomous sting like their jellyfish cousins.

ACTIVITY: What can you find out about the corals known as gorgonians? How are they different from reef-building corals?

CHAPTER 27

REEF LIFE

A reef provides food and shelter for thousands of different species of fish and invertebrates. The presence of these small creatures attracts larger fish, octopuses, and sharks. Indeed, coral reefs are havens for marine wildlife.

DEADLY COLOURS

Coral is brightly coloured, as are the creatures that live in the reef. The reef's festive appearance contrasts with its inhabitants' deadly and serious preoccupation: food. The reef animals' colours help them hide amid the coral, either to avoid detection by hunters or to escape being noticed by prey.

CLOWN FISH

This colourful fish has no need to hide itself away, because it has a better form of protection. The clown fish lives among the stinging tentacles of the sea anemone, feeding on the algae that stick to these tentacles. It appears to be immune to the anemone's venom, perhaps because it is covered in a protective slimy coating.

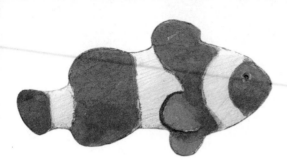

BLACK-SADDLED PUFFER FISH

Although it is only about 4 inches (11 centimetres) long, this small reef fish has little to fear from most predators. Like all puffer fish, when threatened by a hunter it can inflate to twice its normal size. An inflated puffer fish is too much of a mouthful for any but the largest predators.

PARROT FISH

This brightly coloured fish feeds on coral, which it gnaws from the reef with its parrot-like beak. The stony skeletons of the coral pass through the fish's digestive system and end up as fine, silvery sand, which is often found on the ground among reefs.

ACTIVITY: There is a particular type of spiky starfish that devours coral. Can you find out what it is called and draw a sketch of it?

Chapter 28

The Middle Levels

Below a depth of about 660 feet (200 metres), sunlight vanishes from the ocean. The creatures down here are well adapted to life in these waters—some of them even have their own lights to illuminate the darkness. There are no plants at these depths, so each night, millions of animals from the middle levels rise closer to the surface in search of food.

TWILIGHT ZONE

1. Brittle Star
2. Cuttlefish
3. Mackerel Shark
4. Squid
5. Swordfish
6. Leatherback Turtle

Because the waters are dark, predators in the twilight zone need especially powerful senses to find prey. Squid and cuttlefish have large eyes that gather just enough light to see by. Sharks have an excellent sense of smell—they can detect a drop of blood in the water from 1 mile (1.6 kilometres) away.

MIDNIGHT ZONE

Many creatures of the midnight zone are scavengers that feed on a rain of dead animals drifting down from above. The giant squid and sperm whale both live at this depth and are mortal enemies. Huge squid-sucker scars have been found on the bodies of sperm whales—evidence of previous tussles.

MIDNIGHT ZONE

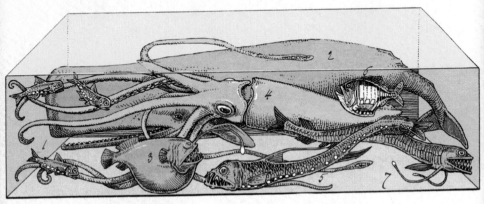

1. Lantern Fish
2. Sperm Whale
3. Anglerfish
4. Giant Squid
5. Viperfish
6. Hatchetfish
7. Dragonfish

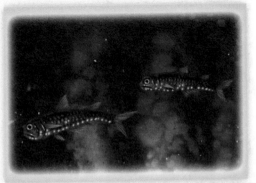

LANTERN FISH

Lantern fish live in large deep-water shoals, where they provide food for many deep-sea predators. Each species of lantern fish has its own unique pattern of lights along its body; males and females use their lights to communicate with each other.

ACTIVITY: Many deep-sea fish have light-producing organs. Can you discover if any land animals make their own light?

Chapter 29
The Ocean Depths

Animals that live at great depths must be able to withstand the enormous pressure from the weight of water above them. Deep-sea creatures can survive at these depths because their bodies are full of water, which cannot be compressed. If their bodies had air pockets, like human bodies do, they would be crushed by the pressure.

ABYSSAL ZONE

1. *Basket Star*
2. *Fangtooth*
3. *Dumbo Octopus*
4. *Sea Cucumber*

The thick mud of the abyssal plain is home to countless marine worms and other burrowing creatures. A variety of soft-bodied animals, such as sea stars and sea cucumbers, crawl and slither across the surface of the plain and are hunted by deep-sea predators.

THE TRENCHES

1. *Deep-water Shrimp*
2. *Vent Clam*
3. *Tube Worm*
4. *Deep-water Mussel*

Deep down at the bottom of the ocean's trenches, the Earth's crust is very thin. Hot gases escape into the water through cracks in the surface known as thermal vents, or "black smokers." The unique environment provided by these vents is home to a variety of animals that appear to live entirely separately from the rest of the ocean's animals.*

> *** PUBLISHER'S NOTE**
> The presence of life at extreme depths was discovered by ROVs (Remotely Operated Vehicles) during the 1970s. It is astounding that Professor Aronnax seems to have been aware of this deep-water life in 1863.

ACTIVITY: The fangtooth has the largest mouth in the ocean for its size. Invent your own deep-sea fish, giving it huge jaws, large eyes, and maybe even a light-tipped lure to attract prey.

Chapter 30

Whales and Whaling

The largest beasts of the sea—whales—are found throughout the world's oceans. These warm-blooded mammals can withstand even the freezing waters of the Arctic and Southern oceans, thanks to a thick layer of insulating blubber beneath their skin. Despite their enormous size, most whales are harmless creatures that feed on tiny, shrimp-like creatures and small fish. Large numbers of these majestic animals are caught and killed by whalers each year, chiefly on account of the valuable oil that can be obtained from their blubber.*

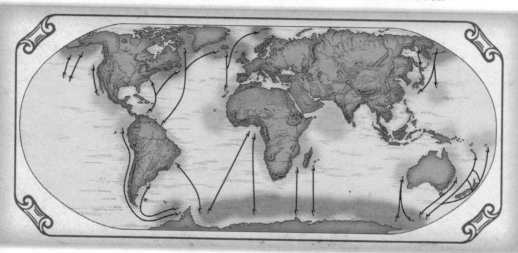

Whale Migration

Through careful observation, those who hunt whales for a living have learned a great deal about their prey. Although whales are generally solitary, they often gather in large groups to undertake great journeys. Humpback whales, for instance, spend the summer feeding in the cool waters around the poles (shown in red). As winter approaches, they form great herds that swim thousands of miles to their winter breeding areas in the tropics (shown in purple). Once their calves are born, the herds swim back to the poles and disperse.

---

* PUBLISHER'S NOTE
Commercial whaling was finally banned under an international treaty of 1986, by which time several species had been hunted almost to extinction.

SURFACE PERIL

Whales are safe beneath the waves. It is only when they come to the surface to breathe that they are vulnerable to whalers. Lookouts on whaling ships constantly scan the waves for "whale signs"—the glimpse of a tail or the distinctive spout of water droplets formed when a whale exhales from its blowhole. When a whale is sighted, the whalers launch small boats from their ship and attack the creature with harpoons (barbed spears).

TOOTH TROPHY

The sperm whale is unique among large whales in that it has teeth; the others have bony plates of a substance called baleen for filtering food from the water. In addition, the skull of a sperm whale contains many gallons of spermaceti: a waxy substance that is used to make the best-quality candles. Whalers who are lucky enough to catch a sperm whale often celebrate their success by carving whaling scenes on the creature's teeth.

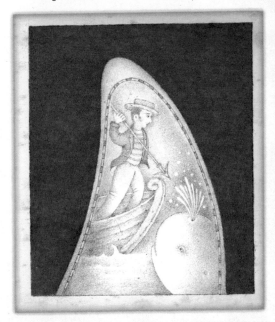

ACTIVITY: Write a sea shanty about a whale. It should rhyme if possible. Try starting with the line "One stormy day our ship set sail."

CHAPTER 31

A WHALE OF A TALE

Moby-Dick is the best book ever written about whaling—in fact, it is probably the best book ever written about the relationship between humans and the oceans. The author, Herman Melville, spent several years working on various ships, so his writing carries the authentic voice of experience.

HERMAN MELVILLE

Herman Melville was born in New York City in 1819. He first went to sea as a cabin boy in 1839, although he did not enjoy the transatlantic voyage to Liverpool. Two years later, however, he joined the crew of a whaling ship that sailed from New Bedford, Massachusetts. The demanding life on board seems to have suited him; he especially enjoyed sailing around the islands of the South Pacific. Later, Melville joined the crew of another whaler as a harpooner and even served briefly in the U.S. Navy. In 1844 he returned to America and began to write books based on his experiences. His first two, *Typee* and *Omoo,* were about island life and won him immediate praise from the critics. His third novel, *Moby-Dick,* is about whaling and has earned him a reputation as one of America's greatest writers.

MOBY-DICK

This book tells the story of the hunt for a single whale—a huge white sperm whale that the sailors call Moby-Dick. There are many strange characters in the tale, including a tattooed harpooner named Queequeg and the storyteller himself, Ishmael. However, the strangest of all is Ahab, captain of the whaling ship *Pequod*. Ahab is obsessed with finding and killing Moby-Dick out of a desire for revenge—the whale bit off Ahab's leg during a previous encounter. The lonely figure of Captain Ahab, his wooden leg tapping endlessly as he paces up and down the deck, dominates the book, which slowly builds to a tremendous finale with a three-sided life-and-death struggle between man, beast, and the sea itself.

ACTIVITY: Can you find and read a copy of *Moby-Dick* from your local library? Be warned: it's a long book with a complicated plot!

CHAPTER 32

CHARLES DARWIN

Despite everything we know about the oceans, there is much more still to be learned. As a result of discoveries made during a five-year round-the-world voyage, the scientist Charles Darwin has developed a most convincing theory as to how life on Earth has developed.

VOYAGE OF THE *BEAGLE*

In 1831 Charles Darwin joined the crew of the *Beagle*, a British surveying ship sent to make charts of the South American coast. Darwin was the ship's naturalist; his job was to collect specimens of all the animals and plants encountered during the voyage. After returning to England, he began writing about everything he had seen. In 1859 he published a book entitled *On the Origin of Species by Means of Natural Selection*, which has revolutionised scientific thinking.

CLASSIFICATION OF SPECIES

The main task of a naturalist is to identify and classify species according to their characteristics (see page 54). During his studies, Darwin has collected hundreds of different specimens to classify. He has caught and stuffed birds, trapped fish and preserved them in vinegar, and even built his own net to capture the ocean's tiniest inhabitants.

GALÁPAGOS FINCHES

Darwin's breakthrough came when he realised that some species differ from others only very slightly. On the Galápagos Islands, for example, the various species of finches differ only in the size and shape of their beaks.

EVOLUTION OF LIFE

According to Darwin, all the plants and animals on Earth have slowly developed, or "evolved," from simple ancestors. Over long periods of time, one group from a species has gradually turned into another species, and so on, eventually producing the bewildering variety of types, shapes, and sizes that we see today. The mechanism behind these transformations is known as "natural selection": those animals that are best suited to a particular environment will flourish, whilst those that are less well-suited will die out.

Solutions

Chapter 3 (p. 15): West-southwest is equivalent to 247.5°.

Chapter 4 (p. 17): "My sails are damaged."

Chapter 7 (p. 23): 75 atmospheres

Chapter 10 (p. 29): Santorini

Chapter 11 (p. 31): *Adventure, Discovery, Endeavour, Resolution*

Chapter 13 (p. 37): 60 feet (18.29 metres)

Chapter 16 (p. 43): The world's biggest tidal range, of 55 feet (17 metres), occurs in the Bay of Fundy, Canada.

Chapter 20 (p. 54): The Swedish scientist Carl Linnaeus (1707–1778)

Chapter 22 (p. 59): Arthropods

Chapter 25 (p. 65): Australia's Great Barrier Reef

Chapter 27 (p. 69): Crown-of-thorns starfish

PUBLISHER'S NOTE

Inside the watertight container within which this book was found, a selection of gummed images was also discovered, presumably intended by Professor Aronnax to be a useful learning aid for readers of the book. The images have been reproduced here by the publisher for the amusement of the young oceanologists of today.

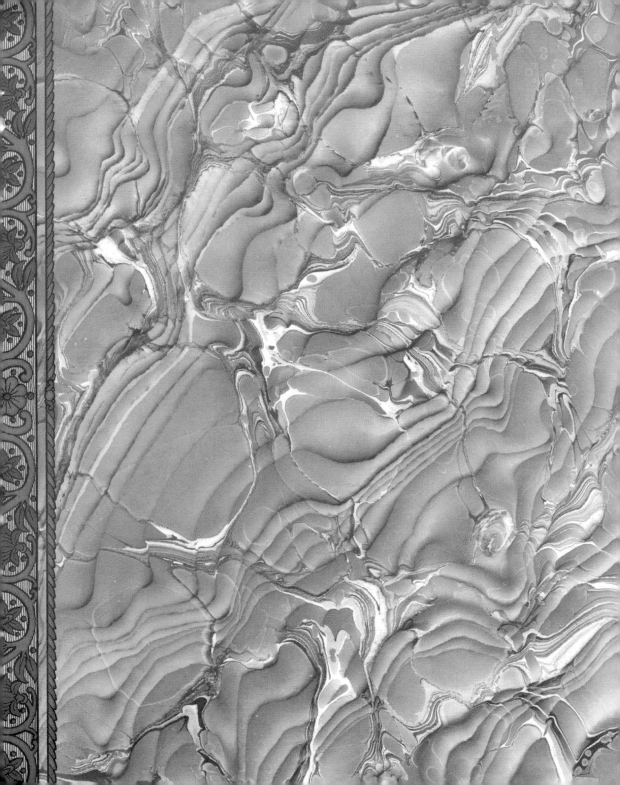